SIX FEET UNDER

INCURSION LEGENDS: BOOK ONE

BRYAN DONIHUE

Edited by
DAVID "SPOOKY" CASSIDAY

Section 28 Publishing

Six Feet Under
Incursion Legends: Book One

Copyright © 2016 by Bryan Donihue. Published by Section 28 Publishing.

All rights reserved. No part of this book may be reproduced in any form or by any means without permission in writing from the publisher, Section 28 Publishing.

Send inquiries to:
Section 28 Publishing
Grand Rapids, Mi 49544
e-mail: bryan@s28.us

Edited by: David "Spooky" Cassiday

This is a work of fiction. All of the characters, events, locations, and governmental agencies portrayed are either fictitious, or are used in a fictitious manner. Any similarity does not reflect the actual person, event, agency or location.

DEDICATION

First and Foremost - Thank you to Jesus Christ for giving me the imagination to create the tales, and a modicum of talent to put them on paper, or in this case, on screen. It may seem incongruous to dedicate a dark urban paranormal novel to Christ, but in the end, HE is the light that shines in the darkness.

This is dedicated to my wife, Christina. She puts up with way too many late nights from me, and supports my weird and annoying writing habits.

To my kids, who miss time with dad while he works on his books. I'm proud of all of you. And Maria, who is probably reading this after bedtime—go to sleep.

To my friend, confidant, and in the best of senses, secretary, David Cassiday. He is my Content and Continuity Editor. Any mistakes left in content or continuity are mine, usually because I ignored his advice.

To my game group in Grand Rapids, you brought these characters to life originally, and cheer me on while I keep them alive.

And finally, to my fans. It is fun and amazing to talk to those of you who genuinely enjoyed the book. Even those who keep asking about the sequels. Keep asking, it helps motivate me to tell the next story. Thank You!

PROLOGUE

Darkness. I love the darkness. It hides all kinds of sins.

The light from the overhead streetlamp formed a small pool in the midst of the darkness cloaking the street—it was the only streetlamp still glowing on this block. This neighborhood was old, and what few businesses remained hid behind steel roll-down barricades for the evening. It was just past midnight, the fabled witching hour, and the streets were almost empty. Any residents who were left in the tenement buildings were sleeping behind locked doors and barred windows.

Three blocks away, another neighborhood was in the middle of an "urban revitalization," which meant that hipsters had decided that the neighborhood contained the requisite charm of old chic and they were steadily moving in to create new, trendy cafes and nightclubs among the row houses that had suddenly quadrupled in value. In that neighborhood, every street light worked, and the area teemed with life.

But not here. If anyone happened to drive through this neighborhood after sunset, they were surely lost. And if they got lost in this neighborhood, I guarantee that their doors would be locked and their windows would be rolled up.

I looked out of the small dormer window in the apartment I currently occupied. I visually searched the block, looking for occupied cars, pedestrians, or neighbors looking out the windows. I found no signs of life. Even Mrs. Parkesian seemed to be huddled inside her own apartment. That nosy old biddy had almost seen me several times, and I knew I would have to be more careful.

Her curtains, like the rest of the curtains I could see, were all closed against the night. I stopped and closed my eyes, listening for the sounds of life around me. I could hear the faint noise of the crowds in the new neighborhood drifting on the still night. Several loud, expensive sounding engines idled and roared from that direction, but no engine noises around here. Listening with my senses wide open, I heard some scurrying in the alley below my perch. It sounded like rats. Maybe two? Three? Not enough to get excited about.

Hearing nothing larger than a rat close to me, I decided it was probably safe to emerge. I grasped the upper windowsill and swung, vaulting up and out of the window, and swinging up onto the roof of the building. I landed in a crouch and paused to make sure my exit went unnoticed. I then stood, slowly, to gaze over the neighborhood. My neighborhood.

I turned toward the newer neighborhood and made my way from rooftop to rooftop. The spans between the buildings were seldom more than fifteen or twenty feet across, and I knew this route well. This was my neighborhood. I knew where I could land from a jump without crashing through into the apartment below, which roofs were strewn with debris where I might trip, and which rooftops were favorite make-out locations for young people.

It was a dark, moonless night, and an overcast sky kept the

stars invisible as well. The low overcast did faintly reflect the lights of the bustling city below, and I could see just fine as I silently loped across the skyline. I could not see in full darkness, my eyes weren't that good. But if I had even the faintest hint of light, my eyes adapted, and I could see well. It was basically the same principle as a night vision camera system, and I still required a small amount of illumination to work with. With tonight's illumination, I could see well, albeit in a monochromatic spectrum. As with a night vision camera, I stopped seeing colors, and everything was a shade of gray in low levels of light.

I was almost two blocks away from what I considered my home when furtive movement caught my eye. I slowed to a halt and squatted. I peered over the edge of the rooftop and looked into the alley below.

Hidden behind a dumpster, a man fidgeted with something in his hands, nervously waving it about himself in small motions. He kept glancing back around the corner of the dumpster toward the street. I could see his lips moving. I knelt and concentrated until I could make out his words.

"No. I don't wanna do it. But if I do, I can get some. Johnny said I needed cash. I can't get green. But they might. I need it, but Johnny's a real dick. He won't give it to me."

I waited. The man's conversation seemed to drift along those lines for a while, so I inspected the man. He was... scruffy. He wore a military surplus Army jacket that was threadbare and worn. It was filthy and stained with several rather dubious looking spots. Underneath the jacket, his dirty t-shirt was stained a dark brown and gray. His pants were long and hung on his gaunt frame, with holes in the knees and worn thin on the thighs. He wore dirty sneakers that looked as if they might have been red at one time. His drawn frame spoke of hard street living, probably helped by the hard narcotics he was currently arguing with himself about.

What caught my attention was the small revolver clutched in his shaking hands. From my vantage point, it looked like a cheap brand that was "chrome plated." If it sold in a gun store for over two hundred dollars, I'd be shocked. Even at Seattle's inflated prices it was a real piece of junk. He kept caressing the gun as if it was his security blanket. And it likely was. After all, it helped this petty thief steal enough to buy his chosen narcotic poison.

He suddenly went still as he saw something that interested him around the edge of the dumpster. I followed his gaze in time to watch two well-dressed young women walk past the end of the alley. As they walked, the one on the left stumbled, almost overbalancing her girlfriend on her other arm. From the stumbling and loud whispering, I noticed that they both were too drunk to be walking alone at night, especially through this neighborhood.

The man below witnessed the same actions, and I looked back at him in time to see a look of hunger and cunning wash across his face. He licked his lips as if he could taste the drugs he would buy once he rolled these two girls. He stood up and began slowly walking to the end of the alley. I rose and stepped off the rooftop.

The ground was about fifty feet below and seemed to rush up at me. I bent my knees to absorb the impact and felt my feet hit the asphalt. I landed and bent further to absorb the shock, crouched with my hand out on the pavement for support. Any superhero would be proud of that landing. And through it all, the loudest sound I made was the soft rubber soles of my shoes making a dull thud against the pavement. I had landed less than five feet behind the addict.

Even through the haze of desire and addiction, the man heard my landing. He turned around in time to see me rise from my crouch. Seeing the look in my eyes, he hastily raised the revolver and pointed it at my face.

I doubt he had loaded silver bullets in the gun. I could almost guarantee that there were not any of Norbert's special vampire killing rounds in the revolver. And I cannot imagine that he had his bullets bathed in holy water. With that being said, I still did not feel like getting shot tonight. It hurt, and the gunfire would draw too much attention to the area. Besides, I would have to find more new clothes. So I did not get shot.

Even if he were not an addict going through withdrawal, my reflexes would still be faster than his. I lashed out and grabbed the revolver, ripping it out of the guy's hand before he could even register that I had moved. As a followup, I decked him. Hard. I didn't put all my strength into the blow, but I used my boosted strength to give the man an uppercut that rattled his teeth, slammed his skull against the dumpster, and knocked him out cold.

I pocketed the revolver and picked the man up. I tossed him into the dumpster, where he landed on several bags of trash. I dusted myself off, and stepped out of the alley behind the two very drunk, and very oblivious, young women. From twenty feet away, I could smell the odor of expensive booze, arousal, frustration, and... despair. I'm sure a human could have at least smelled the booze.

"Ahem." I cleared my throat.

The young women whirled around, unsteady on her feet. I held my hands up in the universal gesture of peace.

"Ladies, you seem to have wandered far from the club. Are you lost?"

The slightly less inebriated woman slurred, "Nope. I'm sure my car is around here, somewhere. Now back off pal. I'm not looking for a hookup."

I looked around the quiet, empty street and frowned. "Listen, I'm sure you are fine, but your car isn't on this block. I think you took a wrong turn, and should go back to get a cab from the club." I took the time to catch her eyes, concentrated, and fought her willpower through her alcohol induced-haze. Finally, I felt her will slip, and become mine.

I softened my voice and spoke with her, "You know that you went the wrong way. You know that you need to go back to the club and get a cab. And you know that I can be trusted to point you in the right direction."

The young woman was nodding as I spoke. And just because I found it funny I ended with, "These are not the droids you are looking for."

The enthralled woman spoke up, "These are not the droids I'm looking for, and I can trust you to show me how to get back to the club."

I smiled and pointed the way back to the street filled with clubs and cafes, "Go back that direction, until you find the club you were in. There, you will have the bouncer call you a cab."

She beamed a huge smile at me and nodded enthusiastically. She grabbed her friend, and they began to stumble back the way they had come, toward the life and action. As they left, I turned back to the alley and made my way over to the dumpster and the unconscious addict.

I hauled the man out of the dumpster and got my bearings. There was an abandoned factory about two blocks east, and I began heading in that direction. I stuck to the darkened alleys the whole way, carrying the addict over my shoulder in a fireman's carry. When I had to cross streets, I waited in the shadows until I was sure that there were no vehicles or pedestrians about, then sprinted across the street. It was only a few minutes before I arrived at the factory.

I tossed the man over the chain-link fence surrounding the building and followed him with a leap. I picked up his unconscious form in a fireman's carry again and carried him into the heart of the factory, into a special room that hid from all but the most determined searchers. From the outside, the metal door was rusted and stained, with a simple pull handle attached. Affixed to the wall next to the rusted door was a placard that read, "Storage Closet." I took a moment to look around and made sure that I was still alone in this abandoned factory before I grabbed the handle and pushed the door inward.

Although it seemed rusty and decrepit from the outside, the well-oiled hinges swung the door silently open into the awaiting darkness. I stepped through and tossed the man onto the cold cement floor. I turned back around and swung the door closed, pushing a three-inch-thick steel bar into place to lock it. Although I could see perfectly in the pitch black, I enjoyed the terror that usually accompanied my prey when they saw my fangs, so I reached out for the stack of chemlights that I kept on the shelf next to the door and grabbed one, snapping it and shaking to make the chemicals inside react to each other. The sickly green glow lighted the room.

Roughly fifteen feet square, the walls and ceiling were cinder block construction, and the floor was a smooth, polished cement. In the middle of the floor sat a massive sewer drain with the inch-thick bars deep set into the floor, the cross-hatched bars forming a grid with two-inch openings. Through the grate, I could hear the sound of rushing water—one of the larger sewer drains in this section of town.

I heard a moan from the addict as he stirred. Once he pried his eyes open, panic dawned across his face as he took in the solid walls around him. His darting glances finally landed on me. I was crouched down, staring at him. Waiting for him to speak.

He started babbling, "What the... where am I? How did I get here? Who the hell are you?"

I smiled, it was a dark, unsettling smile with just the tips of my fangs showing, and he blanched, his face going white. "You are my dinner guest this evening."

"Wha? Whaddya mean, 'dinner?'"

I leaned forward slowly, motioning as if to tell him a secret. He hesitantly leaned forward, and I reached up and grabbed the back of his head. I grimaced slightly, smelling his fetid breath as I leaned in and whispered in his ear, my voice soft and low, "You."

My fangs elongated. I tilted slightly down and then ripped out his throat before he could even scream. I fed.

After I finished feeding, I looked at the mangled corpse in front of me. The throat was missing, the wrists were shredded, and there was a fist-sized hole in its chest. It would not take an autopsy to notice that the heart was missing. I licked my lips, sated. I would not be hungry for another few days, and my body was already neutralizing the toxins that were in his bloodstream from his long history of drug abuse. I looked at the grate in the floor. The bars were set into a square metal box set in the floor. I tugged at the grate, and it rose up and aside. I looked down into the darkness below and saw water glinting in the harsh green glow of the chemlight.

I grasped the corpse and dropped it into the rushing water below. This line of the sewer was a continually running main trunk that fed beneath the industrial plants in this area. The fast moving water was about three feet deep, and would carry anything dropped into it over three miles away and deposit it in one of the larger trunk lines that fed out to the bay, and then to the sea. Along the way, the body would be battered and beaten by the walls and grates, torn apart by the currents, and eventually end up in the sea, behind a large grate. If anything remained, the crabs would feed on it. I knew that there were other creatures that lived in the sewers further down the stream that would make that entirely unlikely.

I leaped down into the murky water and held my ground against the current. I took the time to clean any trace of the blood from my face and hands, and to wash out my clothes. I knew that I could not go back up top with any trace of the addict on me. I would have to change into the spare suit in my truck before I went into work.

I finished washing myself off and looked at my watch. I had allowed myself to forget about time. It was almost dawn. I hoped that it was raining up above, or I would be the only one walking around in wet clothes.

Yes, I can walk around in daylight, although I do get sunburned easily. In fact, I had a job that I needed to attend. I had let myself be too distracted by hunting, and my boss would not be pleased. This was the second time this month that I was going to be late, and I would probably be reprimanded.

My name is Burt Holstein, but you can call me, "Six." I work for the Department of Homeland Security in a top secret division called Section 28. And I am a vampire.

ONE
AWAKENING

Three Months Ago

I woke up screaming. Then, I realized that I was actually screaming. I was screaming? I watched the master vampire rip my own throat out. How was I screaming?

I tried to raise my hands to my throat, to make sure it was there. I couldn't move my hands. I tried to raise my head to look at my hands and felt a strap across my forehead as I tried and failed to raise it. I began to panic. I tried the straps holding my arms again. They were fastened at the wrist and at the bicep. I kicked my legs, finding them bound the same way, at the ankles and thighs.

I strained my head, trying to raise it to look around the room. I could not even turn my head to look. It felt like the straps were padded, but solid underneath, as if they had a steel core. It felt as though I were strapped to some sort of padded bed, or gurney. I was flat on my back. The ceiling was a metal, riveted steel, with recessed fluorescent lighting behind wire mesh. Looking to the left and right, I saw burnished metal walls. Solid, with no windows or doors visible.

I stopped screaming. Trapped in a metal room, strapped to a table, and the last thing I remembered was the master vampire ripping out my throat. Was I alive? Was I dead? Was this hell?

I swallowed several times, trying to get some moisture in my throat so I could speak. I was finally able to clear my throat and speak up, "Hello? Anyone there?" It sounded as if I had gargled with gravel. Considering that I didn't have a throat before I died, I thought my voice sounded just fine.

What seemed to be a few seconds later, I heard the click of an electronic lock and then the slight hiss of a pneumatic seal breaking on a door as it opened. Careful footsteps entered the room, calm and slow. They sounded like dress shoes, echoing off what seemed to be a metal floor. The door closed again, and I heard the harsh metallic click of the lock re-engaging. The shoes stopped.

My padded table shifted, slowly tilting up to the vertical. As it rose, I found I was staring into the coal-black eyes of a man of medium build dressed in a dark gray pinstripe suit, perfectly pressed. The man looked to be Native American and was familiar to me. He raised his eyebrows as he looked at me and spoke.

"Mister Holstein, it is good to have you with us again. Well, it might be good to have you with us again. You must forgive me if we don't release you. I'm sure you can empathize with our safety precautions."

I tried to feign indifference, as if I were used to being trapped and unable to move, but it came out forced, "Sure, Boss. I understand that you strapped me to a table in a giant steel cell." I couldn't hold it in any longer, and I lost all pretense of calm, my voice rising, "Seriously, boss. What the ever-f'n hell? What is going on? Where is my team?"

I was getting upset, and that would not help me at all. I tried to reign in my emotions and wait for Agent Smith to continue.

He paused, his eyes boring into me, examining me as if I were under a microscope. Agent Smith seemed to be thinking about how he would continue. He finally made a decision, and nodding to himself, he began again. His calm, cultured voice was soft, "Mister Holstein, you died five days ago at the hands of that master vampire. Your coffin was buried yesterday during a private ceremony attended by your team, and you were posthumously awarded the Presidential Medal of Freedom. Fortunately for you, two days ago, before we sealed your coffin, the coroner realized that your throat had grown back, suggesting that you were healing although you were clinically dead. We ran a few tests and took the proper cautions. In doing so, we discovered that you had become Hominus Nocturnae—a vampire."

I again felt the monster's jaws close over my throat, and the phantom pain as my own throat was ripped away. "He ripped my throat out. I remember the pain. And dying. And then nothing. I died."

My boss, the Supervising Agent of Section 28, frowned while nodding, "We think he bled directly into your rather torn open throat. We don't know whether he did it on purpose, or if he were just bleeding out from where you guys shot him. However it happened, you ingested a sizable quantity of his blood, at least enough to infect you in your last few moments of life."

He shifted the direction of the conversation, and his face grew stoic again, "So now we don't know what to do with you. You are now, by definition, a vampire, and as such, under sanction for termination. And yet, you are one of the first team members that we have ever had become vampires, and especially the first of this new breed. Most of the time, their geas burns them out immediately. They usually don't survive the actual transformation.

"What do you think we should do with you?" The senior agent waited for my response.

I was stunned. Section 28 killed vampires. It's what we, or at least they, do. Why am I even still alive? Even now I was feeling the beginnings of the hunger. I knew that I had to feed soon. Could I keep it under control? I just didn't know.

"I don't know, Boss. Even now I'm getting hungry. I can... hear your pulse. I can smell your blood, and it's making me hungry."

Agent Smith, my old boss, raised one eyebrow. "You can hear my pulse? That is impressive. I did not realize that a vampire's senses were that acute. And that does bring up your one, rather glaring, liability to us—your hunger. We have a few questions about the vampire hunger, and their dietary necessities.

"And this presents us with an interesting option. While you are in our custody, we can study you. We can find out precisely what a vampire requires to... live. We can also find out more about this new species of vampire, and what weaknesses we can exploit. Do you feel like being a lab rat?"

I tried to think. Tried to ignore the cuffs biting my wrists and ankles. Tried to ignore the gnawing hunger that was growing inside me. I studied Agent Smith's eyes, his expression, trying to see where the hidden traps were. What was the downside to becoming a lab rat? Was there any real choice in the matter?

"What's in it for me?" I asked Smith. "It sounds like I'm getting poked and prodded and shafted. What do I get out of it?"

Not a trace of emotion showed on his face as he said, "Why, Mister Holstein, you get to live. I thought you understood how that would work. Either you cooperate with us, or your stay of execution is removed. You know that is how we operate. You do not get to live as a vampire without cooperating with us." He pursed his lips and continued, "That brings up the rather uncomfortable question about your original oath and geas. Why did it not burn you up when you turned?"

He continued, but was interrupted by a discreet knock on the chamber door. He walked over and opened it about two feet. I could not see was talking to him, but I heard a woman's soft voice as she murmured to my former boss.

"Sir," she said in a low, clipped tone. "We have a development you need to know about. There's been an incident."

I saw Agent Smith turn toward me, and he flashed an embarrassed grin. "I'm sorry Mister Holstein. I'm being called away. We will continue this conversation in a short while. Meanwhile, I will arrange for some form of food for you."

Smith turned away from me and opened the door wide enough to slip through and then exited. The door closed with the pneumatic hiss of an airlock door. The room lights went out, and my table top tilted back to horizontal. It took me a few seconds to realize that I was still seeing the room, only now in black and white. I closed my eyes and willed myself to sleep as my mind was racing with the possibilities.

I AWOKE WITH A START, hearing the now-familiar hiss of the cell door opening and noted that the lights were back on. I turned my head to look, and saw a man in full surgical gear, facemask included, walking toward me, carrying two large implements that looked like turkey basters filled with a dark red substance. Blood. Once I figured out what it was, I realized that I could smell it.

I looked at the door and watched as a second person stepped into the room. This was one of the Special Security Services officers that worked security at Section 28. Black BDUs and tactical gear festooned with magazines and grenades were under the thick body armor, and a balaclava and goggles hid his identity under the full SWAT helmet. As he stepped in, he raised a submachine gun to his shoulder and aimed it directly at me. I noticed it was a suppressed MP5 variant and then noticed that I could actually see the rifling in the barrel. Not a detail I enjoyed seeing. My eyes traveled from the gun barrel to the chest, where the name tag should be. It read "Simmons."

I remember meeting Simmons during my brief stay at the compound. He was one of the tactical security team leaders. He was pure warrior, and, if my memory serves me right, he used to be a Navy SEAL. My voice was harsh, even to my ears, "Harry? Is that you?"

The man in the black tactical gear stiffened slightly, but the muzzle of the subgun never wavered. After a pause that seemed to last forever, he finally spoke, his voice tight, "Yeah, Six. It's me. You're not going to make me use this thing, are you?"

I knew how fast I used to be. I had a pretty good idea how fast my new existence made me. And I still did not believe that I was fast enough to beat Harry to the draw. The muzzle of the submachine gun had never moved away from my head. I shook my head.

"No, Harry. I'm not that stupid." I could sense that he relaxed slightly, so I turned to the medic walking toward me.

"So, doc, what's in the turkey basters?" The man startled when I talked to him.

He looked at the two tools in his hands and back to me. "Mister Holstein, I'm Doctor Ward. I have two different types of blood for you to try. We're trying to feed you, and, simultaneously, figure out what exactly are your dietary requirements."

He stopped when he stepped up to my table. With him standing over me, the smell of the blood was overwhelming, with a slight hint of stale onions. The doctor needed a breath mint.

He raised one of the bulbs full of blood and said, "This one contains human blood, type O-negative. We harvested it from a blood bank earlier." He raised the other one, "And this one contains a synthetic human hemoglobin and plasma. Still in the experimental phases, but it has shown a great promise. Now if you will cooperate and open your mouth."

He raised the synthetic blood and stopped, he looked back at me and asked, "Do you have a preference for today? You will need to try both."

I licked my lips, the hunger driving me to distraction. I nodded to the synthetic blood. "Let's try that one. It would be nice to find out I didn't have to kill anyone to live." The doctor nodded and raised the container of synthetic blood to my waiting mouth.

As the first drops hit my mouth, I gagged. It smelled fine when it was in the tube, but the taste was foul. It tasted like the doctor had let an egg salad sandwich spoil in a car that baked in the Texas sun for at least a month, then pureed the results to a consistency of glue. I swallowed the first mouthful, and the moment it hit my gullet, it made the reverse trip, exploding violently back up and out.

Dr. Ward must have been watching my face because he quickly jumped back, avoiding the worst of the violent upheaval. A small part of it landed on his scrubs, but the rest splattered all over me and my table. Simmons made a gagging sound, but bravely held his post. I was impressed that he didn't move. Well, he didn't move much.

I hacked and spit the nasty concoction out of my mouth, my gut still quivering with the violent reaction. Once I was done, I looked at the good doctor and grimaced. "So I would call that a resounding 'no'." He nodded and raised the next container. I nodded and waited.

I closed my eyes as the doctor poured the blood into my mouth. It was cold. It was ok. I had a hint of some underlying chemicals— was this guy on meds when he donated? I swallowed the blood, and it stayed down. Over all, though, it was just... bland. No real flavor, other than the normal coppery taste. No real spices.

I felt my body respond to the blood. It was weird. I felt as if I had just taken a massive jolt of caffeine. My metabolism went into overdrive. I looked at the doctor and nodded, "I think this will stay down. I can feel my energy returning as if my body is leeching the energy from the blood itself. The only downside is that it's simply bland."

He said, "Good. So your body seems to process actual human blood?" He waited for my nod, "Good. I'll categorize the notes later. Are you still hungry? Still feel the craving?"

"Yeah, doc. Even though I had the blood, it feels like I haven't filled up yet."

The doctor pulls a pen and small notebook out of his scrub pocket and began writing notes and mumbling to himself. I tried to not listen in as it quickly became a rambling that I couldn't hope to understand.

The doctor walked to the door, still muttering and writing. He paused at the threshold and said, "Thank you for your assistance, Mr. Holstein. I'm confidant we'll find a good food supply for you. When we leave the room, I'll turn on the washing functions of the room. You'll get wet, but you'll air dry fairly quickly. We need to get rid of the mess you made." And the doctor walked out the door.

Simmons looked at me and said, "I'm sorry. This will suck. On the flip side, at least you won't be covered in vampire vomit." The door hissed closed after he left.

And then, the water nozzles started spraying cold, slightly antiseptic-smelling water. Simmons was right. It sucked.

TWO
EXPERIMENT

The next couple weeks became a monotonous routine. Trying new food sources and testing the limits of my new vampire biology became a daily routine. I was given different samples of blood, and blood-like substitutes and the results seemed to fall into two options. Either the blood was physically and violently rejected by my body, or I could take some value from it. Unfortunately for me, my body rejected my food far more often than not. I was so disgusted by the rotten offal that I expelled, I began to fondly anticipate the antiseptic showers when I covered myself with regurgitated ichor.

When I could tolerate the blood, it was usually one of three creatures: human, pig, or strangely, rat. Even most primates were incompatible with my new discriminating appetite, and the fact I could drink rat blood was rather disturbing. And the bland taste? It took another week of experiments to figure out that I could only draw full energy from the blood if it had been drawn from a still-living creature. And the closer I consumed the blood to when it was drawn, the more flavor it held. After three long weeks, I knew why vampires drank blood from living victims directly. Fresh blood from a living human was very tasty and had the best energy conversion for my body.

What about other food? Once we figured out I could subside on bloodstocks available to Section 28, they brought me solid foods to try. We soon figured out I could tolerate most raw, unprocessed meats. Any other meat products, or anything that was not an actual meat resulted in an abrupt and uncontrolled expulsion from my system. After four weeks of trial and error, the scientists of Section 28 and I confirmed why the vampires fed on living humans: Fresh human flesh and blood were the best tasting and most nutritious source of energy for vampires.

Four weeks. Four weeks naked and secured to a metal table. A full month of being fed things that would poison my body and then being subjected to icy antiseptic showers to clean up the resulting violent rejection of the food. Every day I suffered experimentation by the same couple scientists, and they were only friendly enough to keep me cooperating. They were all business with their experiments and collecting data.

The only one who actually talked to me as a living, thinking creature was Simmons. He and I had long conversations about my life here, and his life as a guard. As much as he feared my escape and worked to remain vigilante, I believe he also came to pity me. After all, I was strapped to a table, poked and prodded by scientists, and subjected to cruel icy showers daily. I believe that pity caused him to remain at the post, instead of rotating out, and I believe it was his empathy that prompted him to carry on our bull sessions while studiously ignoring my captive state. He's the only one who still treated me as a human being.

After we verified why the vampires in the wild feed the way they do, my captive life got strange. While they had been drawing my own black blood daily, the frequency accelerated. Now, they would draw samples twice or three times a day. And then, my food supply suddenly stopped. I had been receiving fresh human blood every couple days as sustenance, and they quit bringing it. On the third day without being fed, I asked one scientist as he came in for a blood sample. He shrugged and told me they were following orders.

I was beginning to get hungry, and the order to stop my food really pissed me off. No, I didn't retaliate. But, I asked the lab geek to ask Agent Smith to come visit me. About four long, hungry days later he stepped into the room just as the scientist was leaving with his latest sample. Simmons stayed behind to cover his boss.

"Mister Holstein, I understand that you have been asking for me for a few days now." The man was, as always, calm and unshakeable. His perfectly creased and tailored pin stripe suit was reassuringly boring, and he gazed at me through his glasses. He continued in his clipped, cultured voice, "You are probably wondering why you have gone for eight days straight with no feedings. I gave the order eight days ago. This is yet another experiment. Several, really."

I raised my right eyebrow in a Spock-like query. "So... What is this experiment about? Does it have anything to do with the multiple blood draws daily? I'm telling you now, I'm starting to feel the hunger and I can tell my body is actually weakening without the energy replacement."

He looked flatly at me and responded, "Part of the reason is to determine the length of time a vampire can survive without feeding. The other part I cannot tell you, at least not for a little while."

I was really getting upset, and I heard it in creep into my voice when I spoke. Simmons tensed as I growled at my boss, "I've done nothing but cooperate. I'm still strapped to this table. Naked. I get doused with icy showers every day because you force feed me crap I can't digest. I've been a model lab rat."

My voice dropped even lower, "But now you are starving me

for an experiment you cannot tell me about. Maybe I should stop cooperating."

Smith blinked slowly. He turned and walked calmly out of the chamber. As he passed Simmons, my boss waved for the guard to follow him out of the room. Just before the heavy vault door closed, Simmons looked back and offered me a consoling look. Then the door closed, and the icy shower started.

Two hours later, one of the scientists was back to draw more blood. I tensed. I tried to interfere. I tried to frustrate the scientist. Unfortunately, they had earlier added butterfly infusion needles in various veins, each with a reusable valve. He could draw the blood despite me efforts. After the scientist and Simmons left and the hiss of the airtight chamber door finished, I received another icy antiseptic shower.

The next two days were a haze of forced blood draws and ice-cold showers. I lost count after the fourteenth shower. I did not see Agent Smith at all during those two days, and my pleas and threats to see him went unheeded.

On the third day after Smith began torturing me, I had the usual morning blood draw, and cold shower. Or rather, I noticed that I had a shower. I knew that the water was ice-cold because I could feel it. But, I no longer felt the effects of the cold. I felt as though I was starving. Was my body shutting down because of lack of nutrients?

After the morning shower turned off, I heard the water drain out and the pneumatic hiss of the vault door opened. I heard Smith's leather-soled shoes and soon saw him in my peripheral vision. I turned my head to stare at him, and I could feel the snarl on my face and the sharp incisors that had suddenly grown into fangs in my mouth.

I also heard the combat boots of Simmons just before he came into view. Smith made a small gesture behind me, and my table slowly rotated up to the reclined vertical position. I felt the blood rush away from my head as I went vertical for the first time in almost a week. After my vision cleared, Smith made sure he got my attention.

"Are you still with us Mister Holstein?" I had never heard this mocking tone come from my boss. I was stunned and couldn't answer as he continued. "Are you still feeling uncooperative with us? You must enjoy those nice frigid showers."

That last bit had me seeing red. Actually, I was suddenly seeing black and white. My eyes had shifted on their own into scary vampire mode, and I watched as Simmons raised his submachine gun to point at my face. I growled out a response, "What the hell are you playing at. I don't deserve to be tortured like this. It's a damn good thing I'm strapped down right now, because you wouldn't make it out of the chamber."

Smith turned to Simmons, whose finger was inching toward the trigger on his MP5. He said, "Lower your weapon, Lieutenant Simmons. Leave the room and seal the chamber door."

I think you would have actually been able to knock Simmons over with a feather at that moment. He looked from Smith to me and back again. His head kept bobbing between the two of us. He shook his head and said, "Sorry, boss. I don't think I heard you right. You want me to lock you in here with this guy as pissed as he is?"

Smith nodded, and said, "Precisely. Do not fear, I am still being monitored by the control room, and you will be able to get in quick enough if anything untoward happens. I need you to leave."

Simmons protested all the way out the door and then threw in a final threat to me if I tried anything with Agent Smith. Then the large vault door closed, and Smith and I were alone in a sealed room.

I had just decided to start yelling at my cruel former boss when Smith raised a small electronic box to his lips. I recognized the voice control remote for equipment that seemed to be scattered all over Section 28. He paused, and then thumbed the button and softly said, "Teddy Bear."

I heard six different clicks, and suddenly the pressure on my wrists, thighs, and ankles disappeared. I shifted my arms and flexed my hands and wrists. I moved my thighs and almost fell over. I quickly regained my balance and stepped off the small platform that formed the end of the metal table.

"I'm not going back onto that table again," I growled. "You'll have to kill me first. I'm done cooperating until I get some answers."

He stood calmly about four feet away from me. He spoke in a soft, mocking tone, "Well, Mister Holstein? I am alone in the room with you. What are you going to do?"

I heard the airlock hiss of the vault door creeping open and made a decision. I knew that I was fast enough to get to Smith before he even moved. And I knew I was fast enough to get to him and feed on him before Simmons could ever get through the vault door. I would die, but I would die sated and avenged for the torture over the last several days. An animalistic howl ripped out of my throat as I leaped at my tormentor, my former boss, my former friend.

THREE
CHOICES

Time slowed to a crawl. I noticed Agent Smith's eyes widen as I lunged at him. Before he could even begin to back away, my talons were around his arms, and my fangs were at his throat.

Wait. Talons? When did I grow talons? All this flashed through my mind as I paused above my boss' neck. Time returned to normal for me, and I heard his sharp intake of breath just before I leaned in and ripped his throat out.

Or at least I tried to rip his throat out.

I was forcibly stopped, barely an inch from his neck, trying my hardest to rip out my boss' throat, and could move no further. I noticed Agent Smith's lips curl upward in a smile and noticed the heat that was worming its way from my chest outward. I felt the burning spread down my arms and up into my neck and jaw and realized what it was. It was my geas. My oath of service and the magical bond that enforced it was physically stopping me from moving forward. My arms and legs began to shake from the strain, and the burning reach my head. As I began to lose consciousness, I heard the hiss of the airlock door opening and the sound of running boots. Then, I felt the crack-sizzle of a taser and lost the battle for consciousness.

Consciousness slowly returned, and I wondered where I was. The soft sheets and mattress beneath me, and the pillow like a cloud under my head were a drastic change from my prior holding cell. Was this a dream? I opened my eyes and saw a soft, white ceiling, not the stainless steel of the prior weeks. I sat up, wincing in pain from the dual indignities of the geas and the taser. Shaking, I stood, feeling, and then seeing, the plush carpeting below my feet. If this was a dream, I did not want to wake up.

I recognized the bedroom layout from my old team apartment in the barracks. If I was right, that door should be a closet. Yes, with four jumpsuits hanging in closet. I looked down and suddenly realized that I was wearing a t-shirt and sweat pants. So if that is the closet, then this door would be the bathroom. Confirmed. Same basic bathroom, with a few of my brand toiletries on the counter. Was this my old room?

The final door in the room led into a large open plan living room and kitchen. Large, comfortable-looking furniture surrounded an entertainment area with a flat-screen tv. The tile in the kitchen area was a stark contrast to the plush carpeting running throughout the apartment. Overhead lights gleamed off the cabinets and appliances. Looking around, I saw the door that should lead out of the apartment. I strode across and grabbed the handle. The handle refused to turn and there was a small keycard RFID access panel mounted on the wall at shoulder height. I knew it was too good to be true.

I walked back across and sat down to watch television. Just as I clicked the power button on the remote, the lock panel buzzed, and I heard the hiss of another pneumatic seal as the thick steel door swung silently open. I turned to look at the doorway and Agent Smith walked in. Just behind him was Lieutenant

Simmons, holding his submachine gun at a low-ready, waiting for me to make a hostile move. I had a feeling it wouldn't be a taser this time. I was willing to bet that the subgun was loaded with vampire-killing rounds this time.

Smith turned and waved Simmons away. "I'm going to close the door. You stay out there. I have my emergency beacon, and Mister Holstein is still under his esoteric controls. I don't think I will need your assistance today." Before Simmons could answer, my boss closed the only door to the outside, and locked himself in with a monster that wanted to hurt him.

I did want to hurt him. He had tortured me for three days. I was starving because he withheld any fresh blood for the past eleven days, and he was fresh meat. But, I could not touch him.

I had been stunned into unconsciousness when I had attacked him earlier, and it was probably the only thing that saved my life. If they hadn't stunned me, my geas would have fried me from the inside out. I had seen the file footage, and watching a human being driven mad as they spontaneously combusted was far more disturbing than anything I had seen in Iraq.

When I first joined Section 28, I swore and oath and signed a contract that placed a geas over me that gave me certain abilities and rights, while enforcing some very severe penalties for breaking the secrecy of the organization. It also reserved some of its most horrifying penalties for those agents who were dumb enough to try to take down the secret organization—see the aforementioned footage of the human torch.

I looked at Agent Smith and snarled. I stopped, cleared my throat, and forced my anger down before speaking, "So what's the plan now? More torture? Are you just going to starve me out? I'm not in any mood to cooperate with any more of your experiments."

He looked hurt. This was the first time I had seen him show

any emotion other than bored or amused. He sat down as he responded, motioning for me to join him, "Mister Holstein, I though you'd be smart enough to know that all those games are over. I only did what I had to. I needed to find out if your geas is still active after your conversion."

I cut him off, still angry. "So you tortured me? You starved me?"

The moment I asked the questions, I felt foolish. Agent Smith nodded as he saw the dawning comprehension in my eyes. Of course, he had to torture me. He had to drive me mad enough to actually attack him and trigger the safeguards built into the geas. I needed to be pissed enough and hungry enough that I wanted to eat him. When I was finally to my breaking point, he had made himself vulnerable to verify that the geas still held. He didn't send a subordinate in because they might have gotten eaten. He was willing to place himself at risk instead of forcing someone else.

Dammit. I was starting to respect the man again.

I was silent a moment. All my fury was suddenly gone. "I understand. Still a shitty move, but I understand why. You had to make sure that my geas was still in control, and that was the only way possible. I'm a monster, and you had to make sure I was still on a leash." I slumped down onto a chair as the tension and energy driving me drained away.

The leader of the ultra-secret division of Homeland Security called Section 28 showed more concern than I had ever seen him show. It was almost as if he were actually a human like the rest of us. Well, as I used to be.

"I'm glad you understand why I had to torture you, Mister Holstein." Agent Smith was shaking his head as he spoke, "I have never had to intentionally harm one of our agents before now. Even those that have had their loyalties misplaced have always been treated swiftly and fairly. Unfortunately, you are in a unique position.

"With the possibility of other agents succumbing to this, or any other, infection, we have to be sure that their controls are still in place. In fact, this may be much more relevant than even you could know."

He looked at me carefully, as if I were again, still, under his microscope. "Now that we have established that you are, indeed, still possessing your mental faculties, and that you are still bound by your control geas, I have a proposition for you, Mister Holstein." The man raised his left eyebrow quizzically.

I felt myself grin, "I wondered when the other shoe would drop. There is no way you are going to keep me caged in here when I'm still useful to you. Especially now that I am officially dead."

"You are correct Mister Holstein, you are currently, officially dead. However, you are technically still on the payroll under the name 'John Black.'" My boss cracked a dry smile, "I'll admit that I was tempted to use 'Smith,' but I figured there are already enough Smiths running around Section 28. I would rather not live in the Matrix." A small grin acknowledged his own joke.

"As is the Section 28 tradition, I will give you two choices. First option, you can go back into the field. You will be assigned to a DHS office, where you will ostensibly work as a Special Agent on an ICE Joint Terrorism Task Force for the SAC in the office. You will also be operating as a Section Twenty-Eight agent in that city and territory. You will not, under any circumstances, communicate with your former team, or any other personnel you know, unless I give you prior clearance.

"You will likely handle many of the 'special cases' solo, and your supervisor will be highly encouraged to give you discretion on your assignments. If a situation arises that needs a full team intervention, I will transfer you away before the team arrives. You will be sent to a large metropolitan area, where you will find enough special work to keep you busy, and enough of a food supply to keep you well fed." I perked up at that.

I opened my mouth to ask a question, but he continued, without letting me speak, "I know what you are going to ask. And the answer is: choose your meals carefully. Test your geas to see how far it will let you go. I recommend that you start with those street thugs and criminals who will not be missed. The junkies. The muggers. Those who prey on the innocent. If the crime rates go down a little over time, I would call that a win for everyone." I was nodding, and thinking of logistics.

My boss looked at me sternly, "Just don't get sloppy. I can only cover so much, and we cannot afford to you to pop up as a red-level threat, can we?"

I thought about my old teammates being forced to hunt me and shook my head. "I got it, boss. Light snacking, no buffets of locals with families. So what's my other option?"

He shrugged. He waved his hands to encompass my comfortable jail cell and said, "This. You will stay here and be subject to experimentation. The choice is yours." He leaned back in his chair, relaxing slightly, waiting for my response.

I thought about it. A life outside, in the real world, as a Special Agent with a secret job sounded good. It was not as though I would have any kind of social life, anyway. I knew what my skills were, and I could definitely explore my new abilities more by living a real life. Could I keep it together? Would I be able to hold the duality without drawing the ire of my boss in my new job, or the attention of my old team? It sounded like an interesting challenge. I made my choice.

"I'll do it, boss. I'll become your secret agent in a field office elsewhere. So where are you going to send me?"

A knowing smile twitched across the lips of Agent Smith. He reached out his hand to shake mine, "I knew you would make the right decision Mister Holstein. Except it is now Mister Black, isn't it? I have your identity paperwork already completed, with a background built into the system that is similar enough to yours that you should be able to keep it straight. Mister Black is a combat veteran who joined Homeland Security to help fight the bad guys here at home. Excellent marks in training and a rapid promotion in the field brought your name to the top of their list. I'll have Timothy draw up your official transfer papers." Timothy was my boss' administrative assistant. He made sure that the Section 28 hunting teams were well taken care of.

I went over a checklist in my head of things I would need for this extended mission. I asked, "What about gear? Will I have anything available from Norbert? Or Russel? What about re-supply?" Russel was the armorer for Section 28, and Norbert was the resident mad scientist who invented all sorts of useful esoteric gadgets for monster hunting. Without their support, I was adrift up a creek of feces with no method of propulsion.

My boss held up his hands in mock surrender, "Norbert and Russel both know of your new status, and have prepared special care packages for you. Your new equipment will meet you at your new assignment, and you can contact Norbert or Russel through your SSP for re-supply."

He continued, "We've also secured a residence in the downtown area for you. If the location works well, you can use it as long as you wish. If you need to move, call Timothy, and he will get you taken care of." He thought of a few more things and counted them off on his fingers. "I'll also have logistics draw a basic clothing package for you. In your paperwork is your initial spending money and several company credit cards. You know the rules. Timothy took the liberty of setting up a bank account for you in your new home city. Is there anything else?"

I was overwhelmed, but knew that things would be sorted out

rapidly. I thought for a moment and asked, "When do I leave and where am I going? You never told me."

Agent Smith chuckled, "You should know better by now Mister Black. You leave for Seattle, Washington in two hours. And you do not even need to take the glitter."

FOUR
FLIGHT

Two hours later, I boarded the Section 28 jet, a Cessna Citation X, and relaxed in one of the available leather recliners. A few minutes later, Timothy climbed aboard carrying a briefcase. He looked at me and smiled as we exchanged warm greetings. He sat in a leather chair across from mine and motioned for the steward. He told the steward we were ready to leave as soon as the tower cleared the plane for taxi and takeoff. Scant moments later, the jet was climbing for the cruising altitude and Timothy was pulling various envelopes out of his briefcase.

My boss' assistant handed me a folder with the word "CLASSIFIED" stamped across the front and a weird series of symbols scattered around the borders. Recognizing the script as some of the warding used in Section 28, I gingerly opened the folder, hoping the wards and sigils would recognize me and not fry me where I sat. I worked through the background and information of my new persona, Mr. John Black.

I complimented Timothy on his work to put this background together. He smiled as I read on. Although I was slightly worried about living up to the high marks during the academy and testing for DHS placement, the listed combat experience could easily explain any combat skills I possessed. When I was satisfied I had my new background memorized, I perused the other documents and personal effects.

Timothy handed me a large sealed envelope marked "PERSONAL EFFECTS" and surrounded by the same runic design. When I ripped it open and dumped the contents onto the table in front of me, I found a wallet, a set of keys, and a folded piece of paper. A New York State driver's license, complete with cheesy photograph, was tucked into the simple wallet. Also inside were several credit cards. All of them provided and paid for by Section 28, though only two of them read as government issue. In the cash slot were ten crisp hundred-dollar bills. Those I would have to break into real spending money quickly.

The keyring held a remote key fob marked with the Chevrolet emblem and a simple house key. I raised my head and looked at Timothy. "What are the keys for?"

Timothy pointed to the Chevy key, and said, "That will be to your government-issued Suburban. It's an older model, but it has blacked out windows and a government plate. In other words, it announces to everyone that you are, in fact, a federal officer. Since this is effectively a covert op, Agent Smith would not give you another War Wagon. However, I know Russel added enough armor to protect you from small arms fire, and Norbert added a few wards that should protect you from most mundane or esoteric threats. There are also a couple different hidden caches in the cargo compartment that contain a variety of gear you might need, courtesy of Norbert and Russel.

"The other key is a key to your small apartment in a rather-depressed section of town. You will occupy the top floor of the building. The building has underground covered parking available, which should protect your truck while you sleep. The note there is your address. All the utilities were opened in your name, and you should be able to have the proofs required to change your driver's license within the next couple months."

I nodded my thanks and stood up. I put the wallet in my back pocket and dropped the keys into my front pants pocket. As I sat down he was drawing another sealed envelope out of the briefcase. This one was emblazoned with the words "OFFICIAL EFFECTS" in red and sealed with the same set of runes that covered the other two.

I tore open the envelope and out dropped a pair of credentials folios and a familiar looking cell phone. I scooped up the Section 28 SSP, a secure-link smart phone that provides secure communications with Section 28, and contained a few custom app suites designed by some of the craziest esoteric research guys in the world. Those would provide a nasty surprise for anyone who was their target. I pressed my thumb to the bottom, and it powered up, announcing my security clearance and opening the main screen. All the familiar apps were there, along with a few I did not recognize. I knew I would have to explore it later. I set the phone back on the table and looked at the credentials on the table in front of me.

One credential wallets was a black worn leather wallet with a green-embossed logo of Section 28 on the front. As I picked it up, I felt a familiar tingle run through my fingers, as if the leather wallet was somehow a living creature that recognized me as its rightful owner. I opened the credentials and saw my identification card and badge, both glowing a pale, luminescent green. I recognized all the symbols and wards. They all glowed faintly as if welcoming me back. I knew that I could still command its power if I needed. I put it down on the table and picked up the other set of credentials.

This one was in a worn blue leather wallet with the embossed seal of the Department of Homeland Security on the cover. Opening this set, I found the official Homeland Security badge and ID card of one Special Agent Jonathan Black. This one had no glowing runes or power contained in the leather. It was a standard set of credentials for Homeland Security.

I dropped it on the table and looked at Timothy. "I think I understand why I have two sets of credentials, but what is Agent Smith's reasoning?" I asked.

Timothy gestured to my old credentials, "That set is the one and only set that has been bound with your identity and geas. It is powered by your geas and your innate power. The only way that binding dissolves is through the death of the Agent. When you need the full power of Section 28 behind you, and when you need to use your geas' power to force someone's cooperation, you will need this set."

He pointed at the other set on the table. "On the other hand," Timothy began. "This other set is the set that identifies you as Jonathan Black, Special Agent for the Department of Homeland Security. That is the set you will use in your day job as an Agent in Seattle. It doesn't have all the power of your other credentials, but Agent Black was not officially Killed in the Line of Duty."

I nodded and said, "Message received. Now, I have to figure out how to carry both without getting them confused."

Timothy gave a low laugh and nodded, agreeing with me, "Yes, it would not be good for your new SAC to see your old credentials. I'd hate to be forced to call the cleaners."

My fellow passenger then pulled another bundle out of his briefcase. I recognized a paddle holster with a gun already tucked inside it. I started to smile, then frowned a little as I recognized the shape of the handgun.

"That does not look like one of my pistols," I complained.

Timothy handed me the holster, and I drew and cleared the pistol. In my hands was a SIG Sauer P229R in .40 S&W. While I was familiar with the firearm, and could shoot it very well, I never did like the fit and feel of it in my hand. This model was the

"DAK" variant with a trigger that provided the same double-action pull every time it fired. The SIG was a fine gun, but I liked my Beretta M9s better.

He grinned and said, "I know you want to carry your Beretta, but the SIG is the standard issue sidearm for the DHS Special Agent, and you need to blend in. Besides, I've seen your range scores. You'll be fine."

He then handed me three already-filled magazines and a dual magazine pouch that would clip to my belt. I checked to make sure the magazines were fully loaded and then put two into the magazine pouch that would ride on my left side. I stood again and set the paddle of the holster into the waistband on my right side. I moved it around a little, adjusting it for ride comfort. I then picked up the SIG and slid a magazine into its frame and hit the slide release, allowing it to slide forward and chamber a round. I holstered my new agency firearm, mounted the magazine pouch on my left side, and then sat back down.

"I'll admit, it feels right to strap a on a gun."

Timothy smiled and closed the lid to his briefcase. He looked at me and said, "Do you have any questions? Is there anything you think we missed?"

I though for a moment and said, "Yes. Agent Smith said something about a bank account? And what about the paperwork for all the little incidentals?"

He pulled out his own SSP and checked his notes. A moment later, he said, "Ok. The paperwork for the bank account and the other items is all waiting in the cache compartment in your vehicle's trunk." He looked up at me. "Speaking of which, we are not flying into Seattle. We are actually flying into Portland, and you will drive from there. Your new boss was told that you would drive from New York, so you need to actually drive into town. Your truck, and all your goodies have been shipped to the Air National Guard unit stationed at Portland. It arrived this morning and is waiting in a large crate in one of their hangers. We'll open it when we land."

Not having any other questions, I decided it was time for a nap, only to be awakened a short time later as we began our descent into Portland International Airport. We taxied to a remote hanger, to be met by an ANG Humvee full of cargo handlers. I disembarked with my rucksack over my shoulder, carrying my new suit jacket in my hand and Timothy followed me down the stairs.

We walked over to the shipping container sitting in the middle of the empty hanger. My boss' assistant and I walked around the container, inspecting it for signs of tampering or damage. As we walked around, I noticed more of the faint runic symbols guarding the container, with wards placed on the sides, doors, and edges. I suspected there were similar symbols on the top and bottom. After signing for receipt of the container, we motioned for the cargo handlers to leave, letting the sergeant know that he could return to collect the empty container after the agency's plane had taken off again.

Timothy drew a key from his pocket and unlocked the warded padlock that was securing the container. As the doors opened I was confronted with the large grill of the Chevrolet Suburban. The 2006 SUV seemed to take up almost every square inch of the container. With barely a foot to spare between the front and the container doors, there were scant inches of clearance around the truck. It took Timothy and I almost thirty minutes to remove all the tie-downs. Crawling in and around the vehicle was tight and claustrophobic. In the end, my shirt looked like I had wrestled a pack of dogs and lost. It was a good thing I had a jacket to cover up the worst of it until I got to Seattle.

With the tie-downs removed, Timothy climbed onto the truck and in through the open moon roof. He dropped into the driver's seat and turned the key in the ignition. The engine turned over instantly and the big V8 roared to life. He pulled the truck out of the container and parked it in the hanger. We walked around to the back and he showed me where the hidden access ports were for the custom caches. Opening the first, I found a small pile of paperwork on top of several cases of ammunition, both pistol and rifle variants, with several monster-killing types.

When I opened the second compartment, I smiled. Nestled inside custom foam padding were two Beretta M9 pistols and a Colt M4 rifle. I lightly caressed the beautiful guns and could not wait to take the time to break them down and check them very thoroughly that evening. I knew that it would be a pointless effort, as Russel would have already worked over them, but I would tear them down and check them completely because it was my life on the line if they failed.

Timothy game me the address of the SAC office in Seattle, and we shook hands. He wished me luck in my new mission, then he returned to the waiting agency jet. By the time the Citation was throttling up for takeoff, I was off the base and on my way to my new home, Seattle. I settled in for a three-hour drive up the highways of Oregon and Washington.

I arrived in Seattle at 3:12pm according to the Suburban's clock. While I drove up the highway, I had stopped briefly at a rest area to clean myself up and to get some humanity back in my face. As I searched for a place to park, I knew I looked like someone who had driven across the country, but no worse for the wear. I could have simply showed up at the office tomorrow morning, but I decided to stop and introduce myself to my new boss. I wanted to see what he and my coworkers were like.

I found a parking spot about a block away and fed the parking meter. I walked in the afternoon sunlight, slightly uncomfortable, but able to walk without flinching or smoldering thanks to the modified vampire virus DNA. I approached the entrance to the office building and greeted the building security officer in the lobby. I announced myself and showed my new credentials to the bored looking gentleman and he waived me on through to the bank of elevators.

The elevators opened on the twenty-third floor, and I walked out onto the floor. It was decorated in the traditional "modern business" look, with institutional paint, and commercial-grade carpeting. A set of frosted double doors in front of me bore the seal of the Department of Homeland Security. I opened one and walked up to the reception desk.

As I walked up, I flashed the most benign grin I could at her without revealing any fangs, and showed her my badge and credentials. "Hi, Stephanie, is it?" I read her name placard on her desk. "My name is John Black, and I'm supposed to meet SAC Browning. I'm just transferring in from the New York office. Is Special Agent Browning in?"

The woman behind the desk smiled as her eyes widen, taking in my rather-disheveled state. She nodded, "Agent Black, we had heard you were coming, but Ted wasn't sure when you would be here. If you would have a seat, I'll go let him know that you are here. Would you like a cup of coffee?"

I told her she could call me "John," thanked her, and politely declined the coffee. I sat in a seat across from the desk and glanced around my new office. Government-issue waiting room furniture ringed the entry-way. As I looked beyond the waiting area and into the office area, I found that there was nothing remarkable. The same standard "modern business" color schemes adorned the walls and furniture, while cheap generic motivational pictures mingled with bland corporate artwork. I could see several cubicles and a hallway that Stephanie had disappeared down. My fingers tapped a rhythm unconsciously on my knee as I waited.

Stephanie soon came around the corner out of the hallway, leading an older man in a gray power suit. The man's peppered gray hair was thinning on top, belying the onset of his late forties or early fifties. As I rose to greet him, he raised an outstretched hand and we shook, his grip surprisingly strong.

I introduced myself and handed my new boss, Special Agent Theodore "Ted" Browning, my credentials. He looked them over with practiced ease and, apparently satisfied, led me back toward that hallway.

He asked me how my trip across country was as led me into his office, a rather spacious corner office with an outstanding view of downtown Seattle. I told him it seemed shorter than it should have, and he smiled. Closing the door behind me, he gestured for me to sit, and then he dropped into the executive swivel chair behind his desk. He studied me thoughtfully for a few moments.

"Special Agent Jonathan Black. I know that you did not transfer from the New York office, despite what the paperwork and the computers say. So tell me something, who are you and why are you playing in my sandbox?"

FIVE

SEATTLE

I somehow managed to keep the same bland smile on my face as my mind raced, furiously trying to figure out what my new boss' game was. How much did he actually know, and how much was just suspicion?

I let me face drop into a frown and asked, "What do you mean?"

His face turned red and I could see the anger reach his eyes as he responded. His tone dropped, and his voice was much softer. It was the calm before the storm. "Stop the games. Your background checks out, but computer records can be falsified. I know the SAC and several of the New York office agents. None of them have ever heard of you. So, I will ask the question one more time. You will think about your answer very carefully. If I don't believe that you are being truthful with me, I will arrest you for impersonating a federal officer, hacking, and terrorism. I will then throw you in the darkest hole I have until whoever helped you comes out of hiding. And then, I will arrest them. One. More. Time. Who are you, and what are you doing here?"

I paused. I knew he was serious. And I figured that he

genuinely thought he could do all those things that he threatened. So the question is, how would Agent Smith want me to handle this? If I flashed my real badge, my cover is blown. I'm done here, and possibly anywhere. I would have to impress every agent and worker in this office. I'd miss something, and the cleaners would have to be dispatched. Then, I had an idea.

"May I have a piece of paper and a pen?" I tried to make my voice soft and compliant, but I was not good at compliant.

He handed me a piece of paper, and I wrote a number down on it—my old badge number. I slid it over to him and said, "Call the Law Enforcement Agent Verification line. Don't try your computer, it won't bring up anything. Call the verification number. Give them that badge number. You will get your answer."

He looked at me suspiciously, but reached out for the phone on his desk. He picked it up and dialed the number that law enforcement officers can use to verify Homeland Security agents and activity while in the field. When it was answered, he identified himself, and asked to verify the badge number I had given him.

I leaned back and waited as his call was routed to one of two people, either Agent Smith, or Timothy if Smith was not available. Once he connected, he said, "Hello, the is SAC Theodore Browning of the Seattle office. I have a man in my office who has identified himself as Special Agent Jonathan Black and has given me this badge number as a reference."

I could almost imagine the conversation on the other end. Smith's cool, dry tone was even now reciting top secret acts and clearances, and threatening to treat SAC Browning even worse than what he had threatened of me. Browning's face grew pale as he listened. He began subconsciously nodding into the phone as if the person on the other end could see him.

He spoke again, the anger having left his voice to be replaced with docility, "Yes, sir. Absolutely, sir. I understand completely, and will make Agent Black welcome in my office. Thank you, sir, and good day to you." Browning hung up the phone and stared at it for a moment.

He raised his head up and looked me in the eyes again, "So, according to the senior agent I spoke with, you are definitely Special Agent Jonathan Black, recently transferred out of a successful tenure at the New Your office, and I should be thankful to have you on my staff."

He shook his head slowly, "I'll hand it to you Agent Black; you have some very powerful people watching over you. I also understand you will be working solo cases from time-to-time?"

I nodded. I needed to patch this up quickly. I would need this man and his entire team on my side if I were going to work both sides of my mission. So I gave my best conciliatory tone and said, "SAC Browning, I'm not here to interfere with you or your team. I am here to work for you, on your team. I assure you that I have earned the right to be a Special Agent for the Homeland Security Investigations, and I will not be a detriment to your team.

"The truth is that I do have a lot of very valuable experience I can bring to your team. The combat experiences listed in my background are actually understated. I might occasionally have to work a solo case where I cannot answer too many questions; however, I expect those to be few and far between. Those cases are absolutely Homeland Security related, but they will have such a high clearance that I will not be able to tell you about them. Can we call a truce and start over?" I reached out my hand to shake his.

He hesitated, made a decision, and stood, reaching to shake my hand. "SAC Theodore Browning, but you can call me 'Ted.' It's great to meet you."

I smiled and hoped that this would be the end of it. "Special

Agent Jonathan Black, sir. It's great to meet you. Please, call me 'John.'"

"Welcome to Seattle, John. Let me take you around to the rest of the team and get you assigned to your new desk. I'll also have Stephanie get your office badge squared away, and your parking pass and codes to the office."

As he walked out from behind his desk, he grabbed the piece of paper I had written my badge number on and dropped it into the large shredder sitting by his desk. I listened as the paper got chewed up and spit out, relieved that he had been the one to do so. We walked out, and I spent the next couple hours orienting myself to the office and my new team. I begged off the trip to the bar with my new coworkers, citing travel weariness, and promised to join them the next time.

As I entered my new apartment that night, I realized that I was hungry. Starving, really. I hadn't eaten anything, or anyone, for several days, and was worried that I might attack someone without planning for all the contingencies. I need not have worried, I found a sealed box in my refrigerator with a note that read, "I thought this might tide you over until you can make arrangements - T."

I tore open the box and found four bags of blood inside the box. I popped the top off one bag and took a small sip. It was older, had that unpleasant aftertaste of being too long dead, but it was still palatable. I drank the rest of that bag and the contents of a second bag before I felt better. With the two bags I ate, and the two remaining, I knew I had about eight days to figure out how I would feed, and not become hunted. I spent the rest of the night unpacking and arranging my apartment.

The next day I began working at the office. While I had never worked at a DHS field office before, my stint in the military and as a private government contractor had taught me all about bureaucracy. I was a little soft on the law enforcement procedures, but I spent much of my time taking notes learning on the job. That first week was fairly intense, but I soon found the same rhythm that the rest of my new team was using, and I could contribute to their work.

During the days, I worked in the office, or in the field as needed. At night, the city was mine. Because I needed only an hour of sleep each night, I could spend countless hours roaming throughout the city. Sometimes I took my agency truck, but more often I walked or rode the public transportation system. I learned about the city. I found out which neighborhoods were likely to be plagued with thugs and criminals, and which neighborhoods had the criminals that hid behind corporate titles and $1,000 per hour lawyers. In my explorations, I was always looking for a way to dispose of any of my victims, and any of the monsters I hunted.

At the end of that first week, I went with my coworkers to a local dive bar that law enforcement patronized. As a vampire, I could not eat and drink normal foods. Instead, I would claim to be full and pass on any food. I did discover something that we never tested back at Section 28, my digestive system could actually handle most alcohol without rebelling. In my nightly forays around the city, I had discovered one new benefit to being a vampire. My body rapidly metabolizes alcohol so that I can never get drunk, so when my fellow agents decided to have a nightcap, I simply went along to participate.

As everyone else went home for the evening, I decided to take another walk. It was about eleven o'clock at night, and I purposefully walked away from the crowded bars and trendy cafes. As I entered an industrial area, I heard footsteps behind me. There were two people, about a hundred yards behind me, and keeping my pace. I made a few more random turns, and the footsteps stayed behind me, although they were gradually getting closer.

I reached a cross street and looked to my right. There was a stretch of pavement in front of an abandoned industrial plant that had four of the streetlights around it out. If the two gentlemen behind me were going to make a move, this would be it. We were away from any well-traveled road, and any buildings still in use were only occupied during the day. I led them to the perfect opportunity.

As I passed beneath the first broken streetlamp, I heard their footsteps speed up a little. I estimated they were only about thirty yards behind me, and closing in very fast. I knew that the next broken streetlamp would draw them to me, so I slowed down. I concentrated, listening to the pair as they stalked me. I heard the ragged breathing of one who was winded, and the other was wheezing badly, with a fluid gurgle when he inhaled. That one had pneumonia. With the breeze at my back, they were upwind of me. Their combined stench spoke of a long time since their last clean shower, and I caught the faint sour whiff of an infected wound.

As I walked into the darker shadow under the broken streetlight, I heard the click of a blade locking into place. I then smelled burnt gunpowder and heard the metallic clockwork of a revolver's hammer being cocked back. I slowed my pace and hunched over, feigning trouble. With a few jogging steps, the two caught up and I heard, "Hey, you. Stop."

I slowly turned, trying to look surprised that these two thugs had accosted me. Looking at them now, I could tell that both were undernourished. They were both likely narcotics users and were only looking to score something to fence so they could feed their habit. The shorter one had a beard and was holding a wicked-looking knife with a four-inch blade. He waved the blade carefully, showing he was familiar with this instrument. The taller one was leaning to the side. The smell of infection was coming from him, and I could see the redness and swelling through the grime on the man's arm. The same arm he was using to awkwardly hold the revolver.

The shorter one spoke with the same voice that had stopped me, "Give us your wallet and your cell phone. Now. I'm not afraid to cut you."

I smiled. There must have been something feral in my expression because I watched the eyes of the shorter one go wide. I could tell that his drug-addled brain was trying to scream all kinds of warnings to his body as I spoke up for the first time. "I don't think so. In fact, I think I'll invite both of you to dinner." I moved.

My monster-fueled muscles, combined with my years of hand-to-hand combat training meant the taller one never knew what hit him. I struck the man squarely on the nose with a punch from my right hand, hard enough to shatter his facial structure. He collapsed before he knew he was hurt.

The shorter man lunged at me with his knife, and if I hadn't been boosted with my monster heritage, he might have cut me. Instead, I stepped to the side and hit him across the throat with my stiffened left hand. As a normal human, this attack has enough force behind it to damage the windpipe. With my vampire strength, this man's neck was crushed back to his spine. He dropped his knife to grab his throat, but I beat him there. I hit him again, jabbing my right fist into his face, again shattering the underlying bone structure. He was falling before his knife hit the pavement.

I stood up and looked around, searching for any witnesses. I took an extra minute to open my senses, listening at all for any human sounds. When I was satisfied that no one saw my kills, I reached down and scooped one under each arm. I looked at the razor wire-topped fence and calculated the distances. Satisfied, I leapt, skimming the wire and landing hard on the other side. I carried my two would-be attackers into the abandoned factory, found a nice, dark place, and fed.

This was the first "live" blood I had ever fed on, and it was amazing. My senses came alive, and I felt the power course through my body. This is why vampires fed on fresh victims—it was for the power. Once I finished, I looked at the two bodies before me. They had all the classic signs of vampire feedings, and the coroner would have a field day, so I knew I had to get rid of the corpses. I listened and heard the sound of rushing water echoing from somewhere deeper in the building, so I went to check it out.

That is how I found my current hide and feeding area. It has access to dump the bodies and has the benefit of being a fairly safe location with an easy emergency exit. I've been very careful about when and where I feed, always making sure to avoid witnesses. It was also only six blocks from my apartment. So far, it seems like the best solution.

The following Monday, I was seated at my desk reviewing a case file for a sting we were conducting. The phone on my desk rang, and as I answered, I heard several telltale clicks of security measures falling into place. I waited.

"Agent Black? This is Timothy. You have an assignment. This is a Priority Yellow, likely fae, probability shows a goblin. Details incoming to your SSP. Good luck."

SIX
BOGGART

After Timothy had wished me luck, he had quickly hung up the phone. Elapsed time was about twenty seconds. Twenty seconds to screw up my week. I pulled out my phone and found the case file from Timothy.

According to the report, an older building in the downtown area had recently been renovated into new, modern office space for the city's prominent tech industry. Strange things had begun to happen after the remodel when the new tenant had taken occupancy. Computers would not work in the morning. Furniture would be rearranged. Files would sometimes go missing. Items would be broken.

This mischief was infrequent and random, never happening in any pattern. With increased building security patrols, and freshly installed CCTV cameras, the businesses believed that they would finally figure out the cause. Instead, the cameras showed nothing. But, when the personnel came to work in the morning, new mischief had still happened overnight.

Only one floor was targeted, and the business offices on that floor were selected in a completely random pattern. There was only one company that leased that floor of the building, but each of their offices had been vandalized at one time or another. The building owners had even called in psychics and mediums to rid the building of the problems, all to no avail.

Analysis estimated that the problem was either goblin (84% probability) or gremlin infestation (15% probability). Since both creatures were fae, and hailed from the Unseelie Court, Section 28 had reached out, but there was no answer from the dark fae court. So I had to figure out who or what was causing the mischief, and figure out how to stop it without breaking a treaty with the Unseelie Court. Should be simple enough.

Logistics had also provided a laptop with a secure connection and an esoteric lock on it for my use in the field, so I logged into the Section 28 archives and began doing background research on goblins and gremlins. I'd seen movies as a kid, but I knew better than to trust any of those movies, so I delved into Section 28's files on the Unseelie Court fae.

As I searched through the archives available, I compared the information on goblins and gremlins, and searched the archives for similar fae. After I finished digging through the records, it seemed as if this might be a goblin, or one of its close kin. I printed abridged copies of the files for reference and enclosed them in specially sealed folders. Each file included either a CCTV image capture or an artist's rendition of the various suspect species for field identification.

I put on my jacket, scooped up the folder, and walked to SAC Browning's office. I knocked on his open door and poked my head in to see whether he was busy. He nodded and waved me into his office, so I walked in and closed the door behind me.

He arched a single eyebrow in a questioning look and spoke, "What's up, John? News on the Tandino case?"

I shook my head negatively, "No, boss. I have to put that on hold or pass it to someone else temporarily. I've been assigned a special case, as we talked about originally."

He pursed his lips. I'm not sure if he had really believed I would be getting extra assignments. "Do you need any support from us?" he asked.

"No thanks. At least not yet. I think this one should be a short case, but I may be out of the office for a few days."

He nodded thoughtfully and said, "Ok then. Let me know if we can help. Give your Tandino files to Karen. She should be able to step in for you."

I nodded and left his office, stopping by Karen Rixon's desk to let her know that Ted was assigning her as lead to the case until I returned. She knew the case we were working on, and could follow up the leads I was working before I received the call from Timothy. I quickly explained what I was working on, then excused myself. I had a long day ahead of me.

I drove out to a specialty electronics store in the suburbs. The one thread that had worked through the entire goblinoid family of fae was the inability to be captured on regular-light spectrum cameras. The files suggested full-spectrum cameras and infrared or thermal-imaging equipment. Full-spectrum cameras accept and record a wider range of light, ranging from the infrared through the visible and up into the ultraviolet spectrum. I didn't know all the technical theory behind it, but this was what the files said would work.

I walked out of the store with a set of sixteen wireless full-spectrum HD video cameras, a set of infrared and ultraviolet lights, and a thermal-imaging system. The entire setup was safely tucked into a large rolling transport cabinet that had a built-in monitor for the cameras. If this was for my current boss, he would can me for blowing budget dollars like this. Fortunately, Agent Smith would not think twice about this expense line.

I drove down to the building in question and parked my

truck. Reaching into the back, I grabbed the trunk full of AV equipment, and another case filled with various lethal and non-lethal equipment for whatever was plaguing this building.

As I strolled into the lobby, I glanced at the large clock on the wall. It was almost three o'clock, and the uniformed security guard behind the desk was watching the traffic in the lobby. I walked briskly over to the security desk and set my cases down. I reached into my pocket and lifted out my Agent Black credentials. Showing them to the guard, I requested to speak with the building manager, a Mr. Isaac Foran.

The guard called the building manager on his phone, and I was soon greeted by a short, rotund gentleman wearing a high-dollar suit and sweating profusely. As we shook hands, I introduced myself, and stated that I would be working on that floor for the next couple nights. I requested a facility maintenance worker to help me install some of the gear I brought with me, and the building manager called to have someone sent from the maintenance office.

As we were waiting for the facilities person, I informed the security guard they were not to come near that floor that evening and informed them they were to stop recording and disable the feeds from the installed security cameras on that floor. I then requested the plans for the current layout of that floor, overlaid with a list of all the security cameras located there. The guard was very helpful and wrote the instructions down for the incoming guards that night.

When the facilities woman arrived, I introduced myself and explained briefly that I would require her help for the next couple hours. Sophie introduced herself and followed me up to the floor in question.

When we arrived on the floor, I wandered around the floor, noticing the placement of each camera and placing a small tag of electrical tape over each lens. As I did so, Sophie followed behind me and assured the business folks I was authorized to work in and around their office and to disable their security system. The few that questioned more vocally were stopped by a simple flash of my credentials. In half an hour we had disabled the entire camera system on this floor and began clearing the floor of business workers.

Sophie and I were able to mount and setup all sixteen cameras throughout the floor while strategically placing the various lights around the open cubicle farm to illuminate whatever the creature was. After almost two hours of hard work, I gathered up the cases, and Sophie and I left the floor, making sure we were the last human beings to leave. I told Sophie that she was done for the day, and that I would take care of things from that moment on. She never complained, but I'm sure she was wondering why we were installing those cameras all over this floor.

I walked over to the security desk in the lobby, only to be greeted by the new night-shift guard. I explained the rules for the night and asked the guard to accompany me up the stairwell up the floor just to make sure that the door onto the floor was unlocked. I asked the guard to carry a chair up the ten flights of stairs to the fifth floor while I easily carried my equipment cases. I made sure the stairwell door was unlocked, and we placed gaffer's tape on the door jams to prevent the door from locking. As he walked back down to his post in the lobby, I opened the camera case and powered up the flat-screen monitor for the cameras. I settled in for a long wait.

According to the time code on the screen, it was 1:34am when I saw movement on one of the cameras. I locked in on the movement and followed the creature from camera to camera across the fifth floor. At one point, it paused and looked directly at one of the new cameras before turning and crawling under a desk. A moment later, I saw a small bit of smoke arise from the computer on top of the desk, and the little creature crawled back out. I got another good look at the creature, and I knew what it was—a boggart.

The boggart was an ugly little humanoid about three feet tall and slightly hunched over as it walked. A large bulbous nose and craggy wrinkles on its face suggested an older creature, and the gnarled teeth and pointed ears announced that it was fae. Dressed in Victorian-era rags, the creature sported a short white beard that looked more tangled than clean. This was almost exactly like the boggart pictured in the Section 28 files.

As I watched the creature move about and create mischief, I quietly opened the file and looked at the intelligence available on the creatures. There were few sources listed, and the Boggart file was very thin. It mentioned that the boggart lives in a magical space between the walls of the building, that they had a sour disposition, and could get mean when confronted. They had evidenced little direct magic, but their glamour and ability to hide were very well documented. Boggarts had to be trapped or attacked in the open, and once they were in their hole, they sealed the door from the outside world.

Like most fae, they were allergic to pure silver, and silver weapons would prove lethal. The files specifically mentioned that once angered, they could not be mollified, and would continue to cause mischief until killed or banished. I now knew that I had to take care of this creature before it hid from the dawn.

I verified where the boggart was causing mischief, silently opened the stairwell door, and crept down the row of cubicles, hoping to surprise the creature while it was mischief making. I stepped around the last cubicle just as the boggart crawled out from underneath another desk. It looked up and saw me, emotions flowing across its face.

I grinned a feral grin and let my fangs show as I greeted it, "And what are you doing here, Mister Boggart?"

If I had been only a human, my life would have ended in that instant. With a speed belying the size and stature of the wizened old creature, it leaped at my face, long, ragged fingernails out-flung for my face, a snarl on its lips, and a growl rumbling from its throat. As a vampire, I watched the creature leap toward me and I sidestepped, drawing the dagger from the small of my back as I did.

A quick reverse swipe across the creature's midsection turned its growl to a scream of agony. As it curled up to protect its wounded midsection, its hands desperately tried to close the long slash that was bleeding profusely, but the wide cut defied its ministrations. I watched as the boggart's eyes rotated up to gaze on me. The anger in its eyes was turning into... fear? It looked at the knife in my right hand, an ancient blade that had delicate runes carved into the blade which were now glowing with a soft blue.

Its eyes slowly shifted back to mine, as it haltingly asked, "Why?"

I kneeled so I could be a little closer, noticing that the wound had appeared to spread, ripping open even as the boggart breathed. I said, "You attacked me, and I had no choice. Why were you here making mischief?" I asked even as the light in the creature's eyes dimmed.

With a final effort, the boggart looked into my eyes and croaked in a scratchy high-pitched voice, "Was mine. Building was mine before was yours." And the boggart died.

As I reached to pick up the boggart's corpse for disposal, the creature grew translucent and vanished. It did not crumble into ash like vampires, but instead it faded away, as if recalled to its home plane.

I tucked away my knife and then went back into the stairwell to collect my cases. I took the rest of the night to carefully collect all the cameras I had installed the prior evening and then remember to remove the electrical tape from the original security camera lenses. At around 8am, I was stowing the final pieces of my gear into my cases when the employees for the fifth floor businesses began arriving. I talked to several people to make sure they understood that their odd troubles should be gone. I made up vague answers about vagrants or large rats, depending on the office worker.

I had just enough time to go back to my apartment and shower before I was due into the office. On my way to the office, I began thinking about the writeup for this case, and how it would take me all day to file the correct paperwork.

It turned out I was correct; it was a long day at the office as I worked on the boggart case file. It was after seven o'clock when I finished the report and closed my laptop. My car was one of only two in the parking garage, and it was a long drive home. I was eagerly awaiting relaxing as I opened the door to my apartment.

Standing in the entry hallway stood three boggarts.

SEVEN
UNLIFE

Three sets of feral eyes stared at me through bushy eyebrows and over large bulbous noses. All three creatures had a snarl on their face, and all three creatures clutched small daggers in their hands. I had witnessed how fast the boggart was when fighting it earlier, and I was not sure about my chances if I had to fight all three at once.

"Hello. Can I ask why you've chosen to invade my home?" I could barely keep the small tremor out of my voice. I think.

The one in front straightened slightly from his hunched postured and addressed me, "We are here because you murdered Knogrash Ivorth." I winced, knowing that bad things happened when boggarts are named. Its voice was a guttural growl. "Last evening you sent him to his ancestors without provocation. We are here to avenge him."

"Wait a minute," I raised my hands to show they were empty. "Before we discuss this, I'm going to slowly reach into my jacket to show you something. It is not a weapon." I reached to my inside pocket and all three creatures tensed, the two in the back crouching lower and taking a couple steps away from their leader.

It was a classic flanking maneuver. Moving even slower, I withdrew my Section 28 credentials.

I opened my credentials and showed them to the boggarts. "Special Agent Burt Holstein. I'm from Section 28." My credentials began to glow a slight green as they verified my identity to the fae in front of me. "Instead of trying to kill each other, let's discuss this like treaty signatories."

The lead boggart nodded and relaxed slightly while its companions slowly stood up from their crouched stance. "What do you want to converse about?" Its low voice growled, tinged with anger, "You are the one who attacked the Unseelie unprovoked. It is you who must take responsibility."

I realized it must be talking about the boggart I dispatched last night. I tried the truth, "My pardon, I did not know the identity of the Unseelie from last night. He attacked me first, I was only defending myself. When I confronted him about the mischief he was causing, he immediately attacked me, without pausing to converse."

The boggart snorted in derision, "You could not defend against one of us, for you are human. You would have to attack him in a cowardly way. Even now you lie to us to preserve your own life." It edged toward me, waving its sharp dagger in front of it.

My smile was tight-lipped, and it paused, not used to my reaction. It remained where it stood, trying to figure out why I was not cowering in fear. I spoke softly, "Your mistake was to believe that I am merely human. Believe me, I am more than capable of defending myself against the likes of you." This time I raised my lips while I smiled, letting my sudden fangs show. I felt my eyeballs shift, and my vision changed to black and white.

The boggart's eyes grew wide as it whispered, "Nightwalker."

I nodded, "Yes, fae. I am not a human who works for Section

28. I am a vampire who hunts for Section 28." I paused to let that sink into him.

The lead boggart was frozen with widened eyes. The two boggarts it was using for backup had also watched me change and were both trembling in fear. Now that I had their attention, I concentrated, breathing deeply to pull my inner monster away from the surface. I felt my fangs retract and my eyes shift to the normal visible spectrum before I began to talk.

"As I was saying, his was a needless death. I was there to find out how we could come to some agreement. Will we be able to come to some mutually beneficial understanding here? Or will it come down to needless violence and mischief? You now know what I am capable of doing."

The lead boggart turned to its two companions, and their voices were low and close, defeating even my sensitive ears as I tried to listen. After a few moments of vigorous discussion, they all turned to look at me, their daggers suddenly tucked into the small sheaths on their belts. The lead boggart again stepped forward, and its voice sounded less like it was gargling with gravel, "I believe that we are open to discussion, if you are willing to provide the venue, here in your house."

I smiled a wry smile, teeth human again, "Absolutely. If you would like to go to the living room area, we can all sit there."

As we walked into the cramped living room, the smile fled my lips. The living room was completely and utterly ransacked. If it could not be opened, it was torn apart. My living room was in shambles, and the lead boggart looked around, and then abruptly began babbling apologies for the state of my house. I worked to keep my anger in check as I realized that they had vented their rage on my home.

I grabbed the only intact dining room chair and dragged it into the living room. The leader of the trio climbed on my ruined sofa opposite me while its two henchmen darted all over the room. I watched them briefly, then realized that they were cleaning up the mess they had made. I squinted, watching them mend the rips in the fabric and the destroyed wood furniture. They were better than any antique restoration expert I had ever seen.

I pulled my attention away from the henchmen and back to their boss. With both of us sitting, we were almost at eye level with each other, and I did not tower over him. I knew I was dealing with fae now, and I had to choose my words carefully. I thought for a moment, and he seemed to be waiting for me to start.

In for a penny, I thought. "Before we begin, I would like to ask some questions, if I may?" The boggart nodded. "Why the sudden intensity of mischief in that building by your fallen kin?"

The growl in the creature's voice intensified, "The renovations of the building destroyed the walls that anchored his home. Once he re-formed the link, he was justifiably upset that his building was destroyed around him. That was his home since the building was raised as he had followed the first tenant from the home country to this city. As is our wont, he wanted to force the occupants to appease him or leave."

The gnarled creature paused, a hint of curiosity in his eye. He continued, "Why were you there? That is neither your home nor work. Why were you interfering?"

It was my turn to pause. I needed to decide how much I was willing to tell these fae who apparently talked to each other about their lives. *In for a pound.*

"This area is now under my control for Section 28. I was assigned to investigate the supernatural mischief at the building, and did so. I expected to find one of your kind, or one of your relations, but I did not desire a confrontation. I merely wanted to solve the issues.

"That brings me to my next question. How can we come to a

nonaggression agreement, just between us? I really do not want to fight you and your kind, and I do not believe that you want to engage me in battle."

The fae grew thoughtful. "I cannot forge any agreements for the whole of the fae, nor for the whole of the Unseelie. I am not in that position of authority." I nodded my acknowledgement. "But I can forge an agreement for myself, and my clan. That will cover all the boggarts in the greater area. Will that be sufficient?"

"It will," I agreed. "As I cannot forge agreements for all of humanity, nor for Section 28, I can give my personal word and bond. Will that be sufficient for you?" It nodded.

I continued, "So can we agree to a nonaggression agreement between us and the parties that we represent? If there are grievances, then you and I will meet to discuss those grievances before any hostilities commence.

"I understand that you and your kin cause mischief where you are bound, and that is your traditional right and way. It is my request that those activities are kept to the normal levels. By keeping to such, there is much less of a chance that my organization will get a call to investigate."

The creature nodded, "It is agreed." It stuck out its small, strong hand to seal the bargain.

I reached out to grasp the proffered hand, "Well and truly agreed." As we shook hands, I felt a distinct energy flow down my arm to my hand, only to be met by a reciprocating energy from the boggart's hand. This was the first time I had made an agreement with a fae, and I now understood why keeping agreements were very important to them. There was power used to bind the agreement. And that power could be used against any who would break the agreement.

I was still marveling at the experience when the creature, my new acquaintance, removed his hand. I cleared my throat, "So how do I contact you if there is a grievance? Or if I need to contact you for a question? You know where my home is, and you know my name. How do I reach you, and what is your name?"

He paused and looked at me hard. "I'll not give you my True Name, if that is your request. But, you may call me 'Trogarth Vestargh.' And to contact me? Simply call my name while you are here. I have linked my home to yours already. I will come when you call. But do not try my patience, Burt Holstein."

I wondered where the dimensional link was and then did not worry about it. I would never find it if they did not want me to find it. I looked up to see the other two boggarts were standing by their now-standing leader. I looked around the room, and what could be repaired, was. Only the electronics were not mended. Even the fae have some limitations.

I said, "Thank you, Trogarth Vestargh, and to your companions. I look forward to our future dealings."

The creature's smile would have scared a London dentist, but the rumble of pleasure was unmistakable. "Indeed, Burt Holstein. I look forward to our future dealings as well." And with that, they turned, walked to a perfectly ordinary spot on my living room wall, melted through it, and faded from view.

I let out a breath and felt my shoulders slump. Normal Homeland Security cases, Section 28 cases, and now apparently I'm making deals with boggarts who are attached to my own house. I wondered if it would ever be easier.

At least my unlife will never be boring.

Finished April 11, 2016.

Thank You!

If you enjoyed this book, please take the time to add a review on the website of the retailer where you purchased this book.

Thank you so much for reading *Six Feet Under*, an Incursion Legends novella. I appreciate your time, and I hope you enjoyed the story. This book is the first in a series chronicling the individual adventures of the members of Section 28 as they fight monsters and try to protect the world. The book is part of the larger series exploring the Hidden Worlds, called Incursion Legends. More information about the Incursion Legends series and the Hidden Worlds can be found online and on Facebook.

Online: IncursionLegends.com
Facebook: facebook.com/incursionlegends

If you want to read about the origin of Six, and the rest of his team, try the first novel in the Knight's Bane Trilogy - *INCURSION: Knightmare*.

Sign up for my World of Incursion newsletter and receive an exclusive short story about a mysterious delivery that threatens Section 28.

Go to: https://bookhip.com/PPJKFG

ALSO BY BRYAN DONIHUE

INCURSION: Knightmare

The Knight's Bane Trilogy—Book 1

Sometimes the barrier that separates our world from others gets thin, and nightmares come through to our world. Team Knightmare is the latest special response team from Section 28 designed to control or eliminate threats from other planes. Their first mission is a vampire hunt. Will it be their last?

INCURSION: Faeblade

The Knight's Bane Trilogy—Book 2

A massacre at a fae nightclub drives the Seelie Court to blame humans. Team Knightmare is sent to Michigan to investigate the horrors, and their job is about to get very difficult. With skepticism from the fae on one side and a group of human monster hunters on the other, Knightmare is trying to stop a war between the fae courts and humanity.

INCURSION: Dragonfire

The Knight's Bane Trilogy—Book 3

Section 28 is the secret agency that is tasked with hunting monsters and with controlling mystical forces that live on our plane. The agency is under attack from forces from Smith's past and from within the United States Government. Can Section 28 survive the attacks? Can Smith?

Pick up ebooks and signed copies of the books at:

IncursionLegends.com/shop

or at Amazon, iBooks, and your favorite retailer.

You can read short stories from the World of Incursion at:

IncursionLegends.com

ABOUT THE AUTHOR

Early in his life, Bryan decided that he would try as many different jobs as possible. Well, it was his high curiosity and low attention span that decided for him. He started in fast food and has worked in sales (retail, used car, business-to-business, door-to-door, credit card processing, vacuum cleaner, and firearms). Bryan has also been a security guard, police officer, and armored car vault manager. And he was a youth pastor.

Eventually, he decided he'd take the "easy path" and become a writer. He was an idiot. Writing is not easy, but it turned out, he was pretty good at it. People seemed to like his stories, so he kept telling them.

Bryan is a published author (fiction and non-fiction), game designer, graphic artist, web designer, consultant, trainer, ministry leader, and multiple-business owner. He is also happily married to his wife of over 20 years, Christina, and father to six or seven kids, depending on the day. He even sleeps occasionally.

Bryan is currently writing from a hidden bunker in Grand Rapids, Michigan. At least that's what he claims. We know he sits in a home office with a brass plaque that reads "Dungeon" affixed over the door.

To read more of the World of Incursion:
IncursionLegends.com
bryan@incursionlegends.com

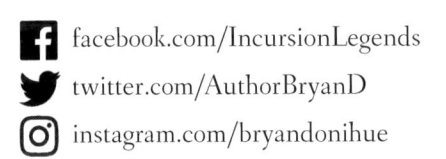

facebook.com/IncursionLegends
twitter.com/AuthorBryanD
instagram.com/bryandonihue

ABOUT SECTION 28 PUBLISHING

Helping Authors Find Their Voice...

Section 28 Publishing is a small, independent press created by author Bryan Donihue to publish his dark paranormal fiction. The fiction published by Section 28 is typically urban fantasy. Currently, Section 28 only publishes works from Bryan, but we are looking forward to working with other authors.

Why "Section 28"?

Originally, the name "Section 28" was created by Troye Gerard, and he graciously allowed Bryan to use the name as a secret government agency in the world that Bryan was creating. The first book set in that world was INCURSION: Knightmare. In that book, "Section 28" is the name of the secret division of Homeland Security that is charged with monitoring and controlling the paranormal in the United States. Bryan chose to use the name as his publishing imprint in homage to that organization, and his first published fiction.

The Mission of Section 28 Publishing

Section 28 Publishing's mission is to help authors figure out the labyrinth that can be independent publishing. From cover design and layout to marketing and sales, Bryan loves to help authors go from a manuscript to a published book that readers want to buy. For an author, nothing is better than having that first fan approach them at a venue, and Bryan wants every author to get that chance.

Made in the USA
Columbia, SC
13 June 2022